Whizz! Bang!

Written by Rebecca Adlard

Illustrated by Keri Green

Collins

Who is in this story?

Listen and say

Tom Teddy

Pink Monkey

Kim Doll

Debra Zebra

Alex

Bobbie Robot

Whizz! Bang! Look! What is this?
Bobbie Robot does not like it.

Whizz! Bang! Look! It is blue.
Bobbie Robot is blue. I like blue.

Whizz! Bang! Look! Pink. I like pink too. Pink Monkey is pink.

Whizz! Bang!

Alex has got a box. Kim Doll
is happy.

Whizz! Bang! Red and green.
Kim Doll you are red and green too.

11

Whizz! Bang!
Red, green, blue, yellow and pink.

Where is Debra Zebra?

Debra Zebra is sad.
Debra Zebra is not yellow.

She is not pink.

Debra Zebra is black and white.

Look, Debra Zebra!
It is black and white.

Debra Zebra is happy now.

Let's go to sleep, toys.

Good night, Debra Zebra.

Picture dictionary

Listen and repeat

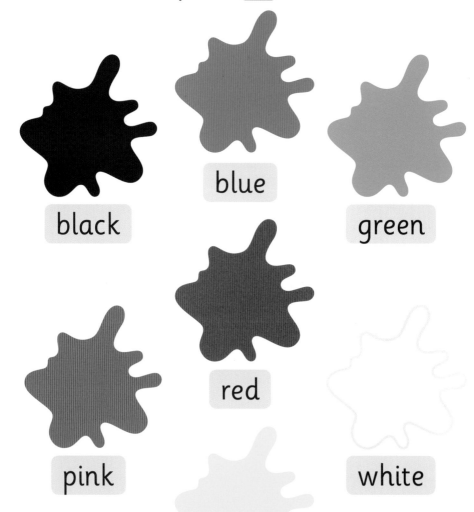

black

blue

green

pink

red

white

yellow

1 Look and order the story

2 Listen and say

Collins

Published by Collins
An imprint of HarperCollins*Publishers*
Westerhill Road
Bishopbriggs
Glasgow
G64 2QT

HarperCollins*Publishers*
1st Floor, Watermarque Building
Ringsend Road
Dublin 4
Ireland

William Collins' dream of knowledge for all began with the publication of his first book in 1819.

A self-educated mill worker, he not only enriched millions of lives, but also founded a flourishing publishing house. Today, staying true to this spirit, Collins books are packed with inspiration, innovation and practical expertise. They place you at the centre of a world of possibility and give you exactly what you need to explore it.

© HarperCollins*Publishers* Limited 2020

10 9 8 7 6 5 4 3 2

ISBN 978-0-00-839810-1

Collins® and COBUILD® are registered trademarks of HarperCollins*Publishers* Limited

www.collins.co.uk/elt

British Library Cataloguing in Publication Data

A catalogue record for this publication is available from the British Library.

Author: Rebecca Adlard
Illustrator: Keri Green (Beehive)
Series editor: Rebecca Adlard
Publishing manager: Lisa Todd
Product managers: Jennifer Hall and Caroline Green
In-house editor: Alma Puts Keren
Project manager: Emily Hooton
Editor: Rebecca Adlard
Proofreaders: Natalie Murray and Michael Lamb
Cover designer: Kevin Robbins
Typesetter: 2Hoots Publishing Services Ltd
Audio produced by id audio, London
Reading guide author: Emma Wilkinson
Production controller: Rachel Weaver
Printed and bound by: GPS Group, Slovenia

Download the audio for this book and a reading guide for parents and teachers at www.collins.co.uk/839810